This Place is a Zoo

By Kyla Steinkraus
Illustrated by Alan Brown

Rourke
Educational Media

A Division of
Carson
Dellosa
Education

www.rourkeeducationalmedia.com

Edited by: Keli Sipperley
Cover and Interior layout by: Rhea Magaro-Wallace
Cover and Interior Illustrations by: Alan Brown
Photo Credit: Page 59 © Liam White / Alamy Stock Photo

Library of Congress PCN Data

This Place is a Zoo / Kyla Steinkraus
 (Paisley Atoms)
 ISBN (hard cover)(alk. paper) 978-1-68191-714-6
 ISBN (soft cover) 978-1-68191-815-0
 ISBN (e-Book) 978-1-68191-910-2
 Library of Congress Control Number: 2016932591

Printed in the United States of America
03-0902311937

Dear Parents and Teachers,

Future world-famous scientist Paisley Atoms and her best friend, Ben Striker, aren't afraid to stir things up in their quests for discovery. Using Paisley's basement as a laboratory, the two are constantly inventing, exploring, and, well, making messes. Paisley has a few bruises to show for their work, too. She wears them like badges of honor.

These fast-paced adventures weave fascinating facts, quotes from real scientists, and explanations for various phenomena into witty dialogue, stealthily boosting your reader's understanding of multiple science topics. From sound waves to dinosaurs, from the sea floor to the moon, Paisley, Ben and the gang are perfect partner resources for a STEAM curriculum.

Each illustrated chapter book includes a science experiment or activity, a biography of a woman in science, jokes, and websites to visit.

In addition, each book also includes online teacher/parent notes with ideas for incorporating the story into a lesson plan. These notes include subject matter, background information, inspiration for maker space activities, comprehension questions, and additional online resources. Notes are available at: www.RourkeEducationalMedia.com.

We hope you enjoy Paisley and her pals as much as we do.

Happy reading,
Rourke Educational Media

Table of Contents

CHAPTER ONE

The Best Field Trip Ever

Paisley Atoms fed her pet Indian gray mongoose his favorite food: a pile of worms. Newton gobbled them up.

She'd been awake since before sunrise. Paisley was always excited to go to school at Roarington Elementary, but today she was even more excited. Today was Mrs. Beaker's annual science class field trip to the Naricorn Zoo. It was the best day of fifth grade!

Paisley couldn't wait. She couldn't wait so badly, she'd been dancing around her bedroom all morning like she had ants in her pants. Of course, if anyone had ants in their pants it would be her best friend, neighbor, and partner in science, Ben Striker. Ben loved ants so much he kept shelves full of ant colonies and worm farms in his closet instead of clothes.

She glanced at the clock. Ben would be over to walk her to school in less than ten minutes. She ran her fingers through her mass of wavy hair and yanked it up into her favorite messy bun. She pulled on her comfy jeans rolled at the ankle, Converse sneakers, and a soft green T-shirt with "I make Horrible Science Puns. But Only Periodically" typed on it beneath a drawing of the periodic table. It cracked her up every time she wore it.

Paisley packed her knapsack with the needed supplies: her favorite Endangered Species of the World book, binoculars, her lunchbox, a pencil, a clipboard, duct tape (you never know), and of course, a pile of fruit snacks, pretzels, and string cheese for Ben, who was always hungry. He usually had dinner twice: once with Paisley and her Dad after they'd tinkered in Paisley's basement laboratory all afternoon, and "second supper" with his own parents after they finished with work.

Newton stuck his head in the knapsack.

"There's no mealworms in there for you," Paisley said. "I'll see you when I get home."

She pressed a new Band-Aid over the cut on her forearm. Yesterday, she and Ben invented a self-driving mower. They even amped up the horsepower so it could get the job done faster. When they tested it on Paisley's overgrown front yard, it worked great—at first. Until the mower's sensors got overloaded and it took off into the Pendlebury's grass, zooming through Mrs. Pendlebury's perfectly manicured bushes and shredding her petunia garden. When they'd finally caught the mower, the Pendlebury's yard looked like a giant crop circle. And not the cool kind. Paisley's ears were still ringing from Mrs. Pendlebury's shrieks of outrage.

"A person who never made a mistake never tried anything new," Paisley said to Newton, quoting her favorite physicist, Albert Einstein.

Newton wrinkled his black nose and chirped at her.

His chirp sounded like a baby bird. Paisley's mom rescued Newton on one of her research trips to India. Mom was a botanist. She was currently in Mexico, researching chocolate cosmos, a beautiful burgundy flower that smelled like chocolate, thought to be extinct in the wild.

Thinking of chocolate made Paisley's stomach growl. She grabbed her knapsack and slung it over her shoulders. She held out her arm for Newton to shimmy up to his favorite perch on her shoulder and followed the scent of Dad's cooking straight into the kitchen. Dad was a biologist and part-time professor at the state university thirty minutes outside of Roarington, aka Boring Town, USA. He was also a fantastic chef, though a very, very messy one.

"Good morning!" Dad said. He flipped a fried egg on the skillet. "I made breakfast chilaquiles." When Mom was gone, they both missed her so much that Dad cooked authentic Mexican food almost every meal.

"Thanks, Dad." Paisley gobbled up breakfast nearly as fast as Newton had inhaled his worms. "Delicious!"

"Have a great day. I can't wait to hear all about it."

Ben knocked on the front door. Paisley waved goodbye as she ran out of the house. She didn't notice Newton slip inside her still-open knapsack.

"Ready?" Ben asked as he adjusted his glasses.

"Ready."

Newton popped his head out, then he quickly tucked himself back inside the knapsack. No one saw him. No one noticed.

"Ready, set, go!" Paisley yelled, and they raced the two blocks to Roarington Elementary. Mrs. Beaker was already herding groups of students onto the bus, calling out last names and checking them off her list.

"Sumi?"

"Here," said Suki with a grin.

"Suki?"

"Here!" said Sumi. She winked at Paisley. Sumi and Suki were identical twins. They had matching chin-length black hair, dark mischievous eyes, and always wore the same clothes, down to their matching beaded bracelets. They exchanged places whenever they could.

Only Paisley somehow knew who was who.

When everyone was on the bus, Mrs. Beaker conducted roll call again. "Always better to be safe than sorry," she said.

"I'd rather be sorry!" Rosalind yelled from the back as her wheelchair was raised by the lift platform. She

loved telling jokes. Paisley helped the bus driver strap the special four-point seat belt around Rosalind and the wheelchair. "What did the bus driver say to the frog?" Rosalind asked. "Hop on!"

"Ha ha," said Mrs. Beaker. The bus lurched out of the school parking lot. The class cheered. "Now, remember, class, we must stick with the buddy system. And you need to have your endangered species scavenger hunt filled out by the time we are ready to return. I will collect your assignments as you get on the bus."

"Is there a prize for finishing first?" Whitney-Raelynn asked, smoothing her already smooth blonde hair.

"Wonderful idea, Whitney-Raelynn," Mrs. Beaker said. "The first place prize winner will be able to skip the next quiz."

Whitney-Raelynn smiled. "Fantabulous. I guess I won't have to study tonight."

Paisley rolled her eyes. Whitney-Raelynn thought she was great at everything. The problem was, she was great at everything. Whitney-Raelynn also had perfectly blonde hair, perfectly fashionable outfits, and a perfectly horrible attitude to match.

"You're so smart, Whitney-Raelynn." Arjun sighed. "The rest of us don't stand a chance." He was over-dramatic about everything. If a pinecone hit him on the head, he'd believe the sky was falling.

"Speak for yourself," Paisley said. "Ben and I intend to win."

"Bring it on," Whitney-Raelynn said. "I'd be happy to wipe the floor with you. Again."

Paisley was about to say something smart back, but Ben tapped her arm. "Look what I brought." He opened the satchel he always carried his field journal in. He pulled out what looked like a Nerf gun. "It's a Cellular Synthesizer Ray. It scans the properties of living creatures and synthesizes their specific skillset."

"Awesome! So you could scan a spider, and the Synthesizer Ray would be able to shoot out a spider web?"

"That's the plan," Ben said. "I just need the right animal to complete my field tests."

The students cheered as the bus pulled into the zoo parking lot. The world's best field trip was about to begin!

CHAPTER TWO

Trouble in Paradise

The students crowded around the entrance to the Naricorn Zoo. Miss Zelda Naricorn handed out maps. Even in her shiny purple heels, she was the shortest adult Paisley had ever seen. Her face looked tired. "Welcome to the Naricorn Zoo, which my father founded fifty years ago this week. We are so happy you could be here today. I apologize in advance that I will not be able to give you a tour in person. We are also having our fiftieth anniversary celebration and fundraiser luncheon this afternoon in the Butterfly Gardens. We have many very special guests, including Mayor Greendale and his daughter, Savannah."

Paisley elbowed Ben. "Savannah Greendale goes to Roarington Elementary. She's in sixth grade."

"I know," Ben whispered back.

"Savannah Greendale is one of my best friends," Whitney-Raelynn announced.

Miss Naricorn cleared her throat. "Please stay out of the Butterfly Gardens, as the caterers are setting up. But the rest of our lovely zoo is yours to explore . . ." Suddenly her voice trailed off. Her eyes filled with tears. "You may be the last group of school children we ever have."

Paisley and Ben looked at each other. What did she mean? Roarington Elementary visited the Naricorn Zoo every single year.

"Are you all right?" Mrs. Beaker asked.

Miss Naricorn sniffled. "I'm so sorry. I don't want to ruin your special day. I just—I'm so—"

"You can tell us," Paisley said gently.

A big, fat tear rolled down Miss Naricorn's cheek. "I'm just so worried. The zoo is completely out of funds. The donations have been less and less each year. I've tried to keep us afloat for so long. But the accountants and the lawyers have informed me that we don't even have the funds to feed the animals. Without money, we have to sell."

The students gasped.

"Sell to who? Will they keep the zoo open?" Paisley asked.

Miss Naricorn pulled a handkerchief out of a pocket in her dress and blew her nose. "That's the worst part. A rich developer wants to buy the zoo's property. He plans to sell the animals, demolish the zoo, and build some fancy condos! It's terrible!"

"Can't you sell to someone else?" Sumi asked.

Miss Naricorn shook her head sadly. "There are no other buyers. The board of trustees will vote tomorrow to sell the zoo. The fundraiser today is our very last hope. The zoo is in desperate need of good publicity and an influx of funds. But the amount of money that would be required"— she snorted into her handkerchief — "is ... enormous."

Paisley patted Miss Naricorn's arm. She didn't know what else to do.

Miss Naricorn cleared her throat and straightened her shoulders. "I want you kids to have the best time of your lives today. After all, the Naricorn Zoo's focus has always been to share with the next generation the wonder and delight of the animal world." With that, Miss Naricorn's face crumpled and she fled into the Zoovenir gift shop.

"Poor Miss Naricorn!" Arjun said.

"Poor zoo animals!" Paisley said.

"Poor us!" Sumi and Suki said. "We love visiting the zoo!"

"Poor me!" Whitney-Raelynn said. "I was planning to have my eleventh birthday bash here in two months. Now what am I going to do?"

Paisley glared at her. "Let's focus on actual problems, okay? All the animals will have to find new homes. And I bet their habitats won't be nearly as nice as Naricorn

Zoo. And where will families go to learn about the animal kingdom?"

"I'm so upset, I can't even think of a joke to say," Rosalind said.

"Okay, class," Mrs. Beaker said, clapping her hands. "While that was very sad news, we still have a fun day ahead of us. We owe it to Miss Naricorn, the animals, and ourselves to enjoy it. Shall we?"

The students picked partners and slowly broke off in different directions. Paisley and Ben were partners, of course, and Suki and Sumi. Arjun joined up with Rosalind.

"Rosalind, do you need any help?" Mrs. Beaker asked. "We're covering a lot of ground today."

Rosalind flexed her powerful arm muscles. She spun her wheelchair in a circle. She kissed her biceps. "You need tickets to view this gun show."

"I believe you! Okay, be safe everyone! We'll meet at the pavilion for lunch."

Whitney-Raelynn stalked off by herself. "I don't need a partner," she muttered. "I'm going to win the competition all by myself."

Ben shook his head as he watched her go. "There goes trouble."

"We have bigger problems to worry about," Paisley said. "Is there any way we can help save the zoo?"

Ben shook his head. "I don't see how."

"We could buy the zoo ourselves," Paisley said.

"Too expensive."

"We could invent a printer to create the money the zoo needs."

"Too illegal."

"We could transport all the animals home and turn our house into a zoo."

"Too impossible."

Paisley sighed. "We've got to come up with something. Science is a way of thinking," she said, quoting the astrophysicist Carl Sagan. "So we just need to think harder. Or science better. Or something."

Rosalind rolled up beside them. "Arjun and I are going to the HISS Herpetarium first. I love snakes. You want to come?"

"Count us in," Ben said.

"Excellent," Rosalind said. "What do you call taking a selfie with a cobra? A misssstake!"

"Very funny," Arjun said. "Look at the third clue. That's gotta be some sort of slimy creature, right?"

They read it together: "This tiny creature stores its poison in its skin. Its rainforest home is rapidly disappearing. It is brightly colored. It lives in groups and eats crickets, ants, and beetles."

Rosalind grinned. "Crunchy! Who wants a beetle sandwich?"

CHAPTER THREE

It's a Zoo Out There!

They walked up a winding path marked by colorful paw prints. The herpetarium was a brick building with no windows. Inside, it was dark and cool. They were the only ones there except for a janitor in jeans and a Naricorn Zoo T-shirt. He was washing out one of the glass enclosures. The walls were covered with panes of glass, each housing various reptiles, amphibians, turtles, and snakes. In one enclosure, a green mamba slithered down a tree branch. In another, a blue spiny lizard basked beneath a sunlamp. A black, red, and yellow banded coral snake coiled on top of a rock.

Other enclosures held tiny, brightly colored frogs. Paisley pointed to a lemon-yellow frog clinging to a jungle leaf. "Here it is. *Phyllobates terribilis*, the golden poison dart frog. They're so deadly, the poison from one frog can kill at least ten adults."

"Imagine if his cage broke on accident," Arjun said. "That little guy could kill all of us!"

"In theory," Paisley said. "But not that one. Poison dart frogs raised in captivity and kept from their natural insect prey never develop poison."

"He's beautiful," Rosalind said. She wrote the answer on their scavenger hunt sheet. "Why are frogs so happy? Because they eat whatever bugs them!"

Ben and Paisley laughed.

"What about this clue?" Rosalind said. "The largest of its kind, this creature moves without legs. It lives in swamps and streams of the Amazon. It eats wild pigs, deer, and even jaguars—which they swallow whole.'"

"Ewww!" Arjun made a face.

Paisley pointed to a massive snake with a greenish

body dotted with dark oval spots. Its terrarium was as tall as the ceiling. "*Eunectes murinus*, the green anaconda. It can reach up to twenty-eight feet long and weigh over five hundred pounds. It constricts—or squeezes—its prey to death."

"I would not want to meet that alone in a jungle," Paisley said. She touched the ancient key she wore on a chain around her neck. The key was a gift from her mother. The key contained a crystal energy that Paisley and Ben used to go on grand adventures. Not even a key with special powers could save you from a snake like that. "Female anacondas will sometimes eat the males."

Rosalind laughed. "That's the most interesting thing I've heard all day!"

"Why's this one empty?" Arjun said. "And this one?" He was looking at a row of several empty terrariums.

The janitor rinsed out his washcloth in a bucket and came over. "That's just temporary. We've taken some of the non-venomous snakes over to the Butterfly Gardens for the fundraiser luncheon. The guests will have the privilege of picking up the snakes and holding them for pictures and such. I guess some people like that kind of thing."

"Thank goodness, I thought they'd escaped and would eat us any second," Arjun said. He was a bit of a worst-case worrier.

"What is a snake's favorite subject?" Rosalind asked the janitor. "Hissss-tory!"

The janitor chuckled. "That's a good one."

Rosalind showed him her paper. "Can you point us in the right direction? The clue is: 'There are only a few of these left in the United States, due to illegal hunting and disappearing habitat. It lives in mangrove swamps and coastal lagoons. A fierce beast, it grows up to fifteen feet long and weighs two thousand pounds.' "

"Sure. Go straight out the other end of the building," the janitor said.

They followed Rosalind through a long, winding hallway and out the herpetarium's back doors. Everyone blinked in the bright sunlight. The Gator Island exhibit was a small island surrounded by murky water. Leathery snouts poked above the surface of the pond. Five or six huge crocodiles lay baking in the sun. They were so still, they looked like statues.

"How can you tell the difference between alligators and crocodiles?" Arjun asked.

"American alligators aren't endangered," Paisley said. "They're all over Florida, according to my Aunt Mildred. *Crocodylus acutus*, or the American crocodile, has a longer, thinner snout and two long teeth that you can see even when its mouth is closed."

"They aren't doing anything fun," Rosalind complained. "You think they'd move if I threw a few stones at them?"

"I wouldn't," Paisley said. There was a large white sign in front of the gator exhibit. Paisley read it aloud: "Those who throw objects at crocodiles will be asked to retrieve them."

Rosalind laughed. "Oh, fine. You win. What's a crocodile's favorite drink? Gator-ade!"

"They look like they're smiling," Arjun said. "Why are their mouths open like that?"

"They're imagining eating you," Ben said.

"Actually, crocodiles sweat through their mouths," Paisley said. "But they could also be imagining you as dinner."

Arjun shivered. "I'm ready for some fuzzy, cute animals. No more prehistoric monsters."

Paisley studied the scavenger hunt sheet. "Where to? Wings of the World, the Hippoquarium, Gorilla Forest, or Paws and Claws?"

"Let's figure out the next clue," Ben said. " 'This New Zealand bird is nocturnal. It can climb trees. It has soft green feathers. Less than two hundred exist in the wild.' Any thoughts?"

"I might have an idea," Paisley said. "Let's head to Wings of the World. It's just past Gorilla Forest."

They followed the path. "My stomach feels funny," Ben said to Paisley in a low voice.

"I still feel bad about what Miss Naricorn said, too," Paisley said. "I'm trying not to think about it."

"It's something else," Ben said. "My brain is telling me I'm missing something. But I don't know what."

"Food usually helps. I brought snacks."

Ben stuck his hand inside Paisley's knapsack as she walked. He pulled out a few packages of fruit snacks. "What else do you have in here? I felt something really weird."

Paisley shrugged. "It's possible I haven't cleaned it out since last summer."

"Gross!" Ben wiped his hand on his pants. "It was furry, Paisley! Something is growing mold in your backpack!"

Paisley just grinned at him. "Whatever it is, I'm sure we can turn it into some kind of experiment."

They entered Gorilla Forest. Different species of monkeys, apes, and gorillas were separated in huge enclosures. Each habitat included a large wooden gym with leveled platforms and ropes to swing on. Several rhesus macaque monkeys slept on a platform. One was sitting in the grass next to the glass. He was holding his tail in his furry hands, picking at fleas and eating them. A large white sign was printed with the words: "Caution. Do not throw anything at the monkeys. They may throw things back at you."

"What are they going to throw?" Ben asked.

"Like the sign says, 'things'. Like their poop," Rosalind said, and giggled.

"You are so mature," Ben said.

"Did you know monkeys share ninety-eight percent of the same DNA with humans?" Paisley asked.

Rosalind snorted. "No wonder that one eating his tail looks so much like you, Arjun!"

"You never told me you had a brother here!" Arjun replied.

"Touché!" Rosalind lightly punched Arjun's shoulder. "It's so hot! I need a popsicle to keep me going."

"I saw a popsicle stand next to the Butterfly Gardens," Arjun said. "I'll take you."

Rosalind grinned. "What a gentleman. We'll catch up with you guys after the birdhouse. See you later, alligators!"

CHAPTER FOUR
Alien Encounters

Wings of the World was a giant aviary filled with free-flying birds of glorious colors and plumage. They saw blue hyacinth macaws, scarlet tanagers, and rainbow lorikeets. There were bright yellow goldfinches and bluebirds, and the red-breasted painted bunting. Birds of all sizes and colors flitted and flew and swooped and skimmed the air just above Paisley's head. They alighted in the trees and sang and chirped.

Whitney-Raelynn was standing in the center of the aviary, glaring up at the birds. "None of them will hold still long enough for me to find one that's green. And how am I supposed to tell how soft its feathers are?"

Paisley smiled. "You've got to know where to look." She'd already spotted the Kakapo; the adorable flightless parrot was standing motionless beneath a large elephant palm. Kakapos used their wings for balance, running instead of flying; they climbed trees with their claws and beaks. And they were absolutely adorable.

Paisley pointed at another white sign hung above the aviary door. "Birds poop every fifteen minutes. How long have you been standing here?"

Whitney-Raelynn squealed and ducked, as if she could somehow escape getting pooped on in a room full of flying birds. She narrowed her eyes and glared at Paisley, trying to decide whether she was tricking her. "Never trust Atoms. They make up everything."

Paisley shrugged off Whitney-Raelynn's favorite pun-insult. "Suit yourself. There's a sign right above your head. I'm helping you."

"You could've fooled me," Whitney-Raelynn snapped.

"Doesn't take much to fool you, does it?"

Whitney-Raelynn's face turned tomato-red. "You open your mouth, and all I hear is 'blah blah blah,'" she hissed as Mrs. Beaker entered the aviary.

"Scientists say the universe is made up of neutrons, protons, and electrons. They forgot to mention morons," Paisley retorted.

"Isn't this lovely, ladies?" Mrs. Beaker asked.

"Yes ma'am," Paisley and Whitney-Raelynn answered in their sweetest voices.

When Mrs. Beaker turned away, Whitney-Raelynn rolled her eyes.

Paisley rolled her eyes right back.

"Let's go before you lose your eyeballs," Ben said.

Whitney-Raelynn glared at Paisley and Ben as they left the aviary. When she thought they couldn't see her anymore, Whitney-Raelynn ducked her head and crept around the aviary with her notebook tented over her head.

"That was worth the price of admission," Paisley said with a grin.

Where to next?" Ben asked. "Paws and Claws? I think the third clue might be referring to a snow leopard."

Just then Arjun dashed up the path toward them. Rosalind was just behind him. "There's something—there's a—he's a—" Arjun gasped. His eyes were huge and his voice shook.

"Slow down!" Ben said.

"I saw—we saw—it was—an alien!"

"What?!!" Paisley and Ben yelled together.

Arjun looked terrified. He gulped in mouthfuls of air, unable to speak. Paisley put her hands on his shoulders. "Breathe in. Breathe out. That's it. Okay, good. Now, what happened?"

"I saw—a man. He was walking past us. He was wearing a shabby coat and a vest with pockets all over it, and his hair was long and straggly."

"Okay, keep going," Ben said.

"As he was walking past us, I saw something."

"What? What did you see?"

Arjun closed his eyes. His whole body shook. "His stomach was—moving. Like, wiggling. Like the movie Alien! Paisley, that man had an alien in his belly!"

"I don't think—" Ben started to say.

"The alien is going to pop right out of his insides and eat us!"

Paisley and Ben turned to Rosalind. Her face was pale. "I saw that dude's stomach move, too."

"We're all gonna die!" Arjun wailed.

"Calm down!" Paisley said.

"Did his belly wriggle and squirm?" Ben asked.

Arjun whimpered. "How did you know?"

"That's it!" Ben smacked his own forehead. "The snakes! It's a mistake. The snakes are a mistake!"

"Wait—what?" Paisley looked from Arjun to Ben.

"It's the snakes!"

"That still doesn't help me!" Paisley said. "Tell me what's going on, right now!"

"We're totally in the dark here," Rosalind said. "Even though it's like, daylight."

Ben took off his glasses and rubbed his eyes. "At the HISS Herpetarium. I noticed something wasn't right, but I couldn't put my finger on it. The janitor said the non-venomous snakes were taken to the fundraiser luncheon for the guests to play with. We walked by all the other snakes—a coral snake, a water moccasin, a death adder, a black mamba, and a cobra. I didn't take a close look at the name tags because I already knew what they were. But my brain still saw them. It took until now to make the connection. The snake enclosures were mislabeled."

"What's the big deal about that?" Rosalind asked.

"Let me be clearer. They aren't mislabeled. They have the wrong snakes inside them."

Paisley's mouth fell open. "What?"

"The terrarium labeled 'black mamba' housed a

harmless water snake. The one labeled 'rattlesnake' had a garter snake in it, and the one labeled 'King Cobra' was filled with two non-venomous eastern hognose snakes."

Rosalind's face turned even whiter. "If the harmless snakes are still in the herpetarium—"

Paisley felt a cold chill run up and down her spine. "Then where are the deadly ones?"

"I think we already know the answer," Ben said softly.

"I'm sorry, but what does this have to do with the guy with the alien?" Arjun demanded.

"It wasn't an alien," Paisley said. "That guy's vest was filled with snakes."

Arjun looked like he might faint. Paisley helped him sit down.

"I don't follow completely," Rosalind said. "Why'd he take the snakes? Is he stealing them?"

Paisley shook her head. She felt like she'd swallowed a rock. "He put the deadly snakes in the tanks at the celebration dinner! He's trying to sabotage the fundraiser!"

CHAPTER FIVE

Snakeology 101

"We've got to warn them!" Paisley cried.

"We will," Ben said. "But look—there he is!"

Back up the path they'd just come that morning, they saw a burly man in an oversized, shabby coat entering the HISS Herpetarium.

"I bet he's getting more snakes!" Rosalind said.

"We've got to catch him," Arjun said. "And make sure he's not an alien."

"Shouldn't we tell Miss Naricorn?" Rosalind asked.

Ben and Paisley looked at each other. "If we do that,

everyone will know," Ben said. "The guests will freak out and leave. The bad publicity and lack of money will shut down the zoo for sure. The bad guys will win anyway."

Paisley held up a finger. "If we capture the thief ourselves and keep him somewhere until the fundraiser is over . . . And we make sure no one handles the deadly snakes, without spreading alarm among the guests, then the fundraiser can go on as planned. Easy peasy."

"I think I'm going to be sick," Arjun said.

Ben nodded. "Okay, I'm in. We need a plan, though. We've got to figure out —"

Paisley started up the path. She wasn't giving the bad guy even one more second to escape.

Ben grabbed her arm. "Paisley! We really need a plan this time! No winging it!"

"I do have a plan!" She pointed at Ben's satchel. "The Synthesizer Ray!"

"What about the fundraiser?"

Paisley checked Ben's watch. "Miss Naricorn said the luncheon starts at noon. It's only 11:30 a.m.

44

We can capture this guy and still get to the Butterfly Gardens before the guests start picking up the snakes."

Ben pulled the Synthesizer Ray out of his satchel and handed it to Paisley.

"What in the world is that awesome-looking thing?" Rosalind asked. "And how do I get my hands on one?"

"We'll tell you later," Ben said.

"Okay. What can we do to help?" Rosalind asked.

"Take Arjun to Mrs. Beaker," Paisley said. "He looks terrible."

As if on cue, Arjun moaned. His face was an unfortunate shade of green.

Rosalind rolled her eyes. "I'm finally smack dab in the center of a real adventure, and I'm stuck with babysitting duty."

Paisley yelled "Thank you!" over her shoulder as they raced toward the herpetarium. "I know exactly which amphibian to synthesize first!" She pulled out the ancient key from around her neck and held it to the Synthesizer Ray. She and Ben chanted "Science Alliance!"

"Here goes nothing," Ben said.

They quietly entered the building. The janitor was still washing the glass enclosures. They told him everything. "I thought he looked strange for a zoo employee!" the janitor said.

"We need the Crucifix Toad," Paisley said. She opened the lid and scanned the little yellow toad. The size of a quarter, the toad was dotted with red, white, and black spots that formed a cross shape on its back. "When they're disturbed, they exude a milky-white glue to protect themselves from predators. The glue is as strong as superglue and will stick to anything—metal, cardboard, dry or wet, cold or hot. Okay, we've copied and synthesized his DNA. Let's go."

They raced back out the entrance of the herpetarium. They ran around the outside of the building, passing Gator Island just as the thief was coming out of the exit.

Paisley pointed the Synthesizer Ray and shot a spray of milky glue at the concrete in front of the man. "What do you think you're doing?" He yelled, but he stepped right into the glue. Paisley held her breath as he took another step. Would it work?

"How many times have you tested the Synthesizer?" She whispered.

Ben shrugged. "This is the first time."

"What?!!"

The thief took another step. The white liquid slopped against his shoes.

"Work, work, work," Paisley chanted to herself. She was afraid to take a breath.

The thief tried to lift his foot again, but the super-strong glue had started to set. He struggled to move and lost his balance. He fell to his hands and knees. He tried to yank his hands out, but they were stuck fast. "What's going on?"

Paisley pointed the Ray at him, but she resisted shooting him again. Even though it would be fun. "You sir, are under arrest!"

She turned to Ben. "We need someone to arrest him."

Just then, the twins walked by the herpetarium. "What's all the commotion?" Sumi asked.

"Can you find security guards to arrest this thief?" Paisley asked.

Suki rubbed her hands together. "Of course we can!"

The man looked from Suki to Sumi, then back again. He groaned and shook his head.

"What's wrong? Seeing double?" Suki said. She and Sumi burst into giggles.

Ben looked at his watch. "It's almost noon!"

They raced down the path to the Butterfly Garden, a beautiful garden enclosed on all sides by tall screened-in walls and a screen roof. The garden featured plants and trees that attracted butterflies of all shapes and sizes. Several dozen tables were covered with white linen tablecloths. A spread of fruit and crackers covered one table, and several caterers dressed in white served a line of guests. The snake tables were on the other side of the dining area. A few guests were already there, lifting the tank lids.

Paisley and Ben zigzagged between the tables, trying not to bump into anyone. "Hey!" someone in a tuxedo yelled behind them.

"There's Savannah!" Ben cried. They skidded to a halt just as Savannah turned toward them. She was holding a huge, deadly black mamba.

Paisley's heart hammered in her throat. Her blood turned to ice in her veins. They were too late! "Don't move! That snake is venomous!"

A crowd of onlookers gathered around them. No one spoke or moved. Savannah's smile melted in terror.

The snake's sleek brown head lifted, fangs poised. It was ready to strike!

Paisley felt something lurch and thump against her back. Her knapsack was moving! Sharp little claws gripped her shoulder. Suddenly a gray streak launched through the air, straight at Savannah. It was Newton!

Savannah dropped the snake. The black mamba wound itself around her, then dropped to the ground as it struck at Newton. The mongoose scampered out of reach.

The crowd gasped. "What a curious looking otter," someone said.

Newton darted closer. The snake hissed and struck again. Newton danced back just far enough to avoid the glistening fangs. The snake stared at the mongoose; its black tongue flickered. Newton trotted in circles around the snake, as if daring it to attack.

Savannah stood still as a statue, tears streaming down her cheeks. The black mamba slithered between her legs, whipping its body toward the mongoose. It attacked again, striking so fast its fangs seemed to sink into Newton's gray fur.

Paisley flinched, barely able to watch. What would she do if something happened to Newton, her brave, wonderful pet? Even though she knew a mongoose was immune to most venom, she was still afraid. For a long, terrible second, she didn't know whether he'd been bitten.

Newton ducked and bobbed. He chattered angrily. He was okay!

He danced closer, then dodged away. The snake struck again and again. Finally, the snake swayed, as if exhausted. Lightning fast, Newton dove in for the kill shot. In one swift move, he lunged and bit the back of the snake's head. The snake's body roiled like a rope at a rodeo. It twitched, then lay still.

Paisley sagged in relief. The crowd cheered. Mayor Greendale rushed in and hugged Savannah.

Newton chirped and squeaked. He climbed up Paisley's pants and shirt and nestled into her arms. She stroked his little head. "I love you, I love you, I love you!" she whispered in his ear.

"What a brave weasel!" The mayor said.

Paisley laughed. "Newton is an Indian gray mongoose. Mongooses are known for being fearless snake-fighters. My mongoose is also very curious. He must've snuck into my knapsack this morning. I didn't even know he was there!"

"When I touched his fur, I thought it was a moldy orange," Ben said.

Just then, there was a commotion behind them. Two security guards dragged in the thief. He was covered head to toe in sticky white glue. Rosalind, Arjun, Sumi, and Suki followed behind, big silly grins covering their faces.

"Miss Naricorn," one of the security guards said. "This is the man responsible for attempting to harm your guests."

Miss Naricorn stomped over. She shook her finger in the man's face. Even though she was barely taller than Paisley, she looked fierce as a warrior. "Shame on you! A young girl was nearly killed because of what you did. What do you have to say for yourself?"

"It wasn't me!" he wailed.

The security guard opened the man's vest. A dozen inner pockets held several wriggling, hissing snakes. The crowd gasped.

"Okay, I admit it. It was me!" he stammered. "I'm so sorry, ma'am. My name is Ralph Walton. Arnold Walton, the real estate developer, is my brother. He told me if I sabotaged the fundraiser, he'd cut me in on the proceeds from his condo development. I really am sorry."

Miss Naricorn sniffed and waved her hand. "Sorry for getting caught, more like it. Take him away. The police will take it from here."

Miss Naricorn turned to Paisley and Ben. "Thank you so much."

"Absolutely!" Mayor Greendale boomed. "Paisley Atoms, you and your friends and your abnormally large squirrel have saved the day. And my daughter. How can we ever thank you?"

"You can thank Miss Naricorn and the Zoo," Paisley said. "I've loved this zoo since I was a little kid. Every

year, Roarington Elementary and many other schools show students the beauty and wonder of nature. Some of us may grow up to be zoologists, biologists, marine biologists, and conservationists. We need to preserve nature both for ourselves and the next generation to come. We fight for what we love, and zoos like this inspire our love and appreciation for animals, including endangered species."

Mayor Greendale clapped. Savannah clapped. Then Miss Naricorn and Ben joined in, and soon the entire crowd broke into applause.

Paisley blushed.

"What a wonderful speech from a budding biologist-in-training," Mayor Greendale said. "I couldn't have said it better myself! I for one will be reaching deep into my pockets today in support of the zoo. I hope my friends will do the same."

Most of the guests nodded. Many pulled checkbooks out of pockets and purses. Miss Naricorn beamed with happiness.

"But what about the scavenger hunt?" Whitney-

Raelynn whined, waving her paper in the air. "I finished it first!"

But no one paid any attention to her.

Mayor Greendale clapped Paisley and Ben on their shoulders. "We've set up an honorary table for our hero students. Please, come sit down and partake of some delicious food. Your teacher, your classmates—everyone is invited!"

Newton sat up in Paisley's arms and chattered.

"There's a spot for your weasel, er, otter, I mean—"

"Just call him Newton," Paisley said.

It was a lovely end to a wonderful day at the zoo. Ben had three helpings of lasagna. Newton ate nuts, fruits, and eggs until his little round belly looked ready to pop. By the end of the meal, Miss Naricorn announced that the fundraiser was a smashing success. The zoo raised enough money to pay all their debts, and then some.

"Now that's what I call a field trip!" Paisley said. Newton chirped in happy agreement.

Science Alliance!: Use Glue to Make Slime

We can't produce glue the way the Crucifix Toad does, but we can use store-bought glue to make some really cool slime! You can change up the amount of ingredients to make it more slimy or more like putty.

Materials:
- 8-ounce (237 ml) bottle of Elmers Glue
- Borax (powdered soap)
- mixing bowl
- plastic cup
- spoon
- measuring cup
- food coloring
- half cup (120 ml) warm water

Step 1
Empty entire bottle of glue into the mixing bowl. Fill the empty glue bottle with warm water, put

the lid on, and shake. Pour the glue-water mixture into the bowl and mix.

Step 2

Add food coloring (a drop or two)!

Step 3

Pour warm water into the plastic cup. Add a teaspoon of Borax powder to the water and stir.

Step 4

While stirring the glue in the mixing bowl, slowly add a little bit of the Borax solution at a time. Now, use your hands to mix! Don't stop mixing while slowly adding the Borax solution. Stop as soon as you feel you've made the perfect batch of slime! Or goo! Or putty!

Women in Science

Gorillas are always interesting to watch. As a zoologist, Dian Fossey spent several decades studying endangered gorillas from the 1960s to the 1980s in the mountain forests of Rwanda. She was the world's leading authority on the behavior and physiology of mountain gorillas. Dian wrote about her experiences in the book *Gorillas in the Mist*.

Dian Fossey (1932–1985)

Author Q & A

Q. When did you decide to include Newton the mongoose in *This Place is a Zoo*?

A. This is the story where Newton gets to shine. I knew at the very beginning I wanted him to be the superstar. So I wrote the whole story around Newton saving the mayor's daughter by killing the snake. Which is what mongooses do so well, of course.

Q. What was your favorite part of *This Place is a Zoo*?

A. Well, Newton, of course. But I also loved when Arjun freaks out over the "alien" wriggling around in the thief's belly.

Q. Is it ever hard to come up with plot ideas?

A. Absolutely! But I try to put myself in my character's shoes. So I think, "What would Paisley do next in this situation?" And then she does it, and that furthers the plot along. Sometimes, the characters and I figure things out together.

Silly Science!

What did the snake give to his wife?

A goodnight hiss!

What is an alligator's favorite drink? Gator-Ade!

What kind of key opens a banana?

A mon-key!

Websites to Visit

To learn more about endangered species:

www.konicaminolta.com/kids/
  endangered_animals

Learn more about the mongoose:

http://easyscienceforkids.com/
  all-about-mongooses

Learn about the anaconda:

http://kids.nationalgeographic.com/animals/
  anaconda/#anaconda-swimming.jpg

About the Author

Kyla Steinkraus lives with her husband, two kids, and two spoiled cats in Atlanta, Georgia. She loves going to the zoo with her family, although she usually avoids visiting the snakes. In her free time, she enjoys reading, photography, hiking, traveling, and playing games with her family.

About the Illustrator

Alan Brown's love of comic art, cartoons and drawing has driven him to follow his dreams of becoming an artist. His career as a freelance artist and designer has allowed him to work on a wide range of projects, from magazine illustration and game design to children's books. He's had the good fortune to work on comics such as *Ben 10* and *Bravest Warriors*. Alan lives in Newcastle with his wife, sons and dog.